A Walk on the Tundra

by Rebecca Hainnu and Anna Ziegler

Illustrated by Qin Leng

INHABIT
MEDIA

Inhabit Media Inc. would like to acknowledge the support of the Qikiqtani Inuit Association (QIA). Without their generous support this publication would not have been possible.

Published by Inhabit Media Inc.
www.inhabitmedia.com

Inhabit Media Inc. (Iqaluit), P.O. Box 11125, Iqaluit, Nunavut, X0A 1H0
(Toronto), 191 Eglinton Avenue East, Suite 301, Toronto, Ontario, M4P 1K1

Editors: Neil Christopher, Louise Flaherty, and Kelly Ward
Art Director/Design: Danny Christopher

Plant photographs:
Qijuktaat, Uqaujait: © 2018 Anna Ziegler • Qunguliit: © 2018 Keir Morse
Paunnait: © 2018 Ellen Ziegler • A'aasaaq: © 2018 Shelley Nicholls
Ujjunnak: © 2018 Sandra Critelli

We acknowledge the support of the Canada Council for the Arts for our publishing program.

This project was made possible in part by the Government of Canada.

ISBN: 978-1-77227-185-0

Printed in Canada

Library and Archives Canada Cataloguing in Publication

Hainnu, Rebecca, author
A walk on the tundra / by Rebecca Hainnu and Anna Ziegler ;
illustrated by Qin Leng.

Previously published: 2011.
ISBN 978-1-77227-185-0 (softcover)

1. Tundra ecology--Arctic regions--Juvenile literature. 2. Traditional ecological knowledge--Arctic regions--Juvenile literature. 3. Inuit—Juvenile literature. 4. Tundra plants--Arctic regions--Identification--Juvenile literature.
I. Ziegler, Anna, 1979-, author II. Leng, Qin, illustrator III. Title.

QH541.5.T8H35 2018   j577.5'8609113   C2018-900437-1

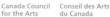

I once read that dedicating a book is an act of love. In the hope of showing even a glimpse of mine to them, I would like to humbly dedicate this book to my parents, Mary and Johanasie Hainnu. At one point in their lives, before foreign materials were available, my parents lived through innovative times. To my mother, who sewed every piece of clothing on my father, and to my father, who provided every meal for my mother through his daily hunting and harvesting. Two best friends who lived traditional lives on the land. Who encouraged their children to attend universities. Who have always shown awesome love to each other and to their children. I dedicate this book to my parents, two individuals who made everything possible for all of us, their children, grandchildren, and great-grandchildren. You are loved, and to us, you have always been the definition of love.

"*Inukuluk Naamajukuluk*"
("dear little person, with all the requirements")

Johanasie Hainnu May 10, 1942–February 2, 2011

LITTLE INUUJAQ flops down on the front steps and sips an orange pop. She looks at the barren hills—the same hills as ever.

"Nothing to *do!*" she sighs. "Boring morning *again.*"

Inuujaq's friends are all asleep. When she tried to visit them, their parents told her to come back later. "They're not awake yet. *Pigaaqtualuuqqaummat*—they stayed out late, so they're not awake yet."

In early August, most kids play outside until the very last light of the long days. But Inuujaq can never join them. Her parents have set a curfew that even her big sister can't escape.

Inuujaq gulps the last of her pop and tosses the can into the ditch.

INUUJAQ'S GRANDMA, Silaaq, comes around the side of the house. She has an old mailbag and a tiny shovel.

"*Anaanatsiaq*, where are you going?" Inuujaq asks. "To the store?" she adds, thinking of candy.

"Out on the land to get *qijuktaat*," Silaaq says. "How about you come along and help me?"

"Walking is so *boring*," Inuujaq thinks. She wants to stay in town and wait for her friends to come out. But she would never say no to her grandma.

She follows her grandma across the dusty road, toward the same old hills.

INUUJAQ WATCHES Silaaq step from rock to rock. Her feet barely touch the land in-between.

Inuujaq tries to copy her. She stretches her legs to reach each rock. There are so many flowers between the rocks! Little ones and big ones. Yellow and purple and pink ones. The sunlight is warm on Inuujaq's arms and the air smells sweet, like licorice.

After a while, Silaaq stops. She closes her eyes and lifts her face to the sun.

"I'm hungry," Inuujaq says.

Her grandma smiles and nods, and keeps walking.

They walk and walk, rock to rock, until Inuujaq can no longer hear the town and her belly begins to grumble.

In town, the other children will be awake soon. Innujaq wonders how far her grandma is taking her.

INUUJAQ WANTS to ask if her grandma has any *palauga* or other snacks to eat.

But, just then, they reach the top of the hill.

"*Tavva*," Silaaq says, "here we are." The hillside is covered in plants, all the way down to a lake that sparkles like blue diamonds.

Silaaq breathes in the lake air. "I used to walk here with *my* anaanatsiaq," she says.

Inuujaq had never thought of her grandma as a little girl before, with a grandma of her own.

SILAAQ BENDS DOWN and picks a funny-looking plant. The leaves are green and heart-shaped, and the tall stems look like red cake sparklers.

"*Qunnguliit*," Silaaq says, "these are qunnguliit." She rubs a few leaves and stems between her palms.

"*Nirilikkit*—eat them," she says, opening her hand to Inuujaq. "*Mamaqtut*. They're good. Especially when you crush them a bit between your palms."

Inuujaq stares at the crumpled leaves.

"Eat *those*? Are they even food?" she thinks. Her belly grumbles again.

"Nirilikkit," her grandma tells her. "They're good for you, Inuujaq."

INUUJAQ INSPECTS one leaf.

She pinches it in front of one eye.

She holds it under her nose.

"In late summer, they're the sweetest," Silaaq coaxes her. "*Niam!*"

Inuujaq puts the little leaf into her mouth.

It doesn't taste too bad, so she chews. Then, her eyes pop wide open and her mouth spreads into a big smile. The leaves are sweet and sour—and *delicious*!

SILAAQ REMEMBERS one summer when her family was hungry for days. Her grandma had fed them a broth made from qunnguliit and their hunger pains went away for a little while.

"Qunnguliit is very nutritious," Silaaq tells Inuujaq. "You can make a broth from it and eat the cooked leaves, too. They give you energy when you are tired."

Inuujaq picks another bunch of stalks and leaves to munch. She jams some into her pocket, too—she can hardly wait to share them with her big sister.

SOON, INUUJAQ and her grandmother are walking across the hills again.

"Where are we going now?" Inuujaq asks.

"To get qijuktaat, just over the next hill," her grandma answers.

Inuujaq's feet are tired. She hopes they find the qijuktaat soon.

"Anaanatsiaq, *why* do you want to cook with qijuktaat so much?" Inuujaq blurts out. "Don't you like the stove at home?"

"Oh, my little *irngutaq*," Silaaq chuckles, "food cooked over qijuktaat is the best food I have ever tasted. You'll always remember it."

And as they walk, Silaaq remembers sitting with her family while her grandma cooked over a fire of qijuktaat. Silaaq thought the smoke smelled delicious. It smelled like hot black tea and sugar.

"The qijuktaat crackles as it burns," Silaaq explains, "and little bits jump into the cooking pot. You'll see."

SOON, SILAAQ and Inuujaq arrive at the other side of the hill. Qijuktaat is everywhere! Its long green fingers and white bell blossoms flutter in the wind.

Inuujaq touches the little branches. They feel prickly on her palms. And they smell fresh, like the summer wind when it comes from the hills.

Together, Silaaq and Inuujaq gather qijuktaat for the cooking fire. Silaaq takes some sacks out of her mailbag. They fill them all and tie them closed.

Inuujaq slings a sack over her shoulder to carry it home.

INUUJAQ SEES the town in the distance. She thinks of filling her hungry belly with *uujuuq* when they get home.

But Silaaq stops walking again. She bends down and picks a small pink blossom.

"This is *a'aasaaq*. My father made tea from this," she says. "I haven't seen this in a long time."

"*Mamaqpa?* Is it yummy?" Inuujaq asks.

"You can make some tonight and find out for yourself! I learned to cook on an *iga* with my mother when I was about your age."

"Me? Cook with my grandma?" Inuujaq thinks. She feels so excited that she hops around in circles like a snow bunting—until Silaaq tells her to help pick more a'aasaaq so that there will be enough for everyone.

"Yes, a spot on the iga for my little Inuujaq," Silaaq says, as they gather the a'aasaaq. "I'll show you how my father liked to brew this tea twice to make it yummy and healthy."

ON THE WAY HOME, Silaaq shows Inuujaq three more plants.

"Try some *ujjunnaq*," Silaaq says, as she eats some herself. "It's mild and a little sweet. See if you like the stems and the leaves. You can also eat the roots."

"This is *paunnait*. Eat the leaves as a snack or to soothe a tummy ache. You can make tea from the leaves and stems, too."

"Now these—niam!" Silaaq says, chewing on a few leaves. "*Uqaujait,* the leaves of Arctic willow. They're delicious with seal fat and berries. You can eat them plain, too, just like this."

"Every plant is special!" Silaaq says happily. "Some are medicine and others are teas, food, tools, building materials, and even chewing gum. Some plants help us predict the weather and guide our direction on the land."

Inuujaq puts her hand in Silaaq's as they walk.

SOON, INUUJAQ sees their little house, bright blue in the evening sunlight. She also sees something shiny in the ditch—her pop can!

"That doesn't belong in the grasses," she thinks. She runs ahead and picks it up. Silaaq smiles.

SILAAQ AND INUUJAQ light a fire. Inuujaq's family comes out to join them.

Inuujaq makes tea for everyone on her grandma's iga. As the a'aasaaq steeps, she rests her head on Silaaq's shoulder. She listens to the qijuktaat crackle and she breathes in its sweet-smelling smoke.

"Anaanatsiaq," Inuujaq says, "may I follow you again when you go out looking for plants?"

"Always, Inuujaq," her grandma says, "always."

Qijuktaat (khee-yook-tat)
English: Arctic White Heather, Arctic Bell Heather • Scientific: *Cassiope tetragona*

• Its long green stems look like braids!
• It has tiny white flowers shaped like bells. They grow at the tips of the stems.
• It grows on hillsides in large patches.

Qijuktaat is used to fuel cooking fires. Its smoke has a delicious aroma and flavours whatever is cooked over it.

Qunnguliit (khoong-oo-leet)
English: Mountain Sorrel, Sweet Leaves • Scientific: *Oxyria digyna*

• Its green leaves are shaped like hearts.
• It has tall red stems that look like cake sparklers. The stems are called *nakait* (nah-ka-eet) in Inuktitut.

Qunnguliit is a special treat to eat! Its nickname is "Arctic candy." The juicy stems and leaves are tangy and sweet. For the best flavour, they should be crushed to mix the juices together. The leaves and stems can be eaten raw. They can also be cooked. Qunnguliit can be eaten all summer, but it is most nutritious and delicious at the end of the summer.

Paunnait (pa-oo-na-eet)
English: Dwarf Fireweed, River Beauty • Scientific: *Chamerion latifolium*

- Its blossoms have four big pink petals.
- Its leaves are long. They are bluish green and they are not shiny.
- Paunnait grow in clusters, often where the soil has shifted. They grow on roadsides, hillsides, and gravelly shores.

The leaves of paunnait have many uses. They can be eaten fresh to soothe an upset stomach. They can also be boiled into a healthy and delicious tea. A very strong paunnait tea can soothe a headache. Collect the leaves at the end of the summer and use them for tea all winter.

Uqaujait (oo-kha-oo-ya-eet)
English: Arctic Willow • Scientific: *Salix arctica*

- Its leaves are bright green with pointed tips.
- It has little hairs in the early summer to keep warm.
- Uqaujait can be spotted by its catkins, which are red in the early summer and then bright white and very fluffy in the late summer.

The leaves can be eaten fresh from the plant. They can also be combined with other ingredients, such as seal fat and berries, to make special dishes. The leaves are also good for tea.

A'aasaaq (ah-ah-sak)
English: Arctic Thrift, Sea Pink • Scientific: *Armeria scabra*

• Its tiny blossoms are pink.

• The blossoms grow in tight clusters of thirty to fifty. They look like one big blossom!

• A'aasaaq consists of long green stems, with leaves growing at the bottom.

The blossoms of a'aasaaq can be used to make a light and fruity tea.

Ujjunnaq (ooj-joon-nakh)
English: Hairy Lousewort • Scientific: *Pedicularis hirsuta*

• Its blossoms are white, pink, and purple. Sometimes they are also yellow and green! The blossoms grow in clusters that spread out over the summer.

• Each blossom has five petals. Two are joined together at the top, and the three at the bottom are flat and wide, which helps insects land on them.

• The green leaves look like they have many small teeth. They are smooth.

Ujjunnaq are good to eat. The blossoms, leaves, and roots can all be eaten fresh.

Glossary of Inuktitut Words and Phrases

Word or Phrase	Pronunciation	Meaning
anaanatsiaq	ah-nah-nat-see-akh	grandmother
iga	ee-gah	stone cooking platform
irngutaq	eer-ngu-takh	grandchild
Mamaqpa?	ma-makh-pah	Does it taste/smell good? Begins with mamaq, which means "taste or smell good."
Mamaqtuq.	ma-makh-tookh	It tastes/smells good. Begins with mamaq, which means "taste or smell good."

Mamaqtut.	ma-makh-toot	They taste/smell good. Begins with mamaq, which means "taste or smell good."
Niam!	nee-um	Yum!
Nirilikkit.	nee-rhee-leek-keet	Eat them. This sentence begins with niri, which means "eat."
palauga	pah-lah-oo-gah	Bannock. A quick bread made from flour, baking powder, and shortening.
Pigaaqtualuuqqa-ummat.	pee-gaakh-too-ah-luukh-kha-oom-mat	Because they stayed out so late.
Tavva.	tab-vah	Here.
uujuuq	oo-yook	Meat that has been boiled.

Contributors

Rebecca Hainnu

Rebecca Hainnu lives in Clyde River, Nunavut, with her daughters, Katelyn and Nikita. Rebecca believes it is important to teach Inuit traditional knowledge about the land, animals, people, history, and philosophies. Her family is usually on the land throughout the seasons. She hopes to pass on some knowledge through her writing. Her work includes *Edible and Medicinal Arctic Plants: An Inuit Elder's Perspective, The Spirit of the Sea, A Walk on the Shoreline, Math Activities for Nunavut Classrooms,* and *Classifying Vertebrates.* Rebecca is an educator in a K–12 school. She was the recipient of the 2016 NTA Award for Teaching Excellence.

Anna Ziegler

Anna Ziegler is the principal of Arctic Willow Consulting, which specializes in program development and evaluation in community wellness, poverty reduction, and adult learning. She has completed graduate research on practices of archiving Inuit traditional knowledge. After living in Iqaluit, Nunavut, for fourteen years, she now resides in Ottawa, Ontario, and works on projects with groups across Inuit Nunangat. She is also the co-author, with Rebecca Hainnu and Aalasi Joamie, of *Edible and Medicinal Arctic Plants: An Inuit Elder's Perspective.*

Qin Leng

Qin Leng was born in Shanghai, China, and lived in France and Montreal, Quebec. She now lives and works as a designer and illustrator in Toronto, Ontario. Her father, an artist himself, was a great influence on her. She grew up surrounded by paintings, and it became second nature for her to express herself through art. She graduated from the Mel Hoppenheim School of Cinema and has received many awards for her animated short films and artwork. Qin has always loved to illustrate the innocence of children and has developed a passion for children's books. She has illustrated numerous picture books for publishers in Canada, the United States, and South Korea.